淘气的乒乓猫

Pim & Pom

家里来客人啦

〔荷〕米斯·博豪宇斯 著　　　〔荷〕菲珀·维斯顿多普 绘　　　蒋佳惠 译

Fiep

人民文学出版社
PEOPLE'S LITERATURE PUBLISHING HOUSE

乒乒和乓乓在阁楼上。

Pim and Pom are in the attic.

今天，女主人的两个外甥女要来玩。
乒乒和兵兵赶忙把玩具摆放好。

The Lady's two little nieces are coming over to play today.
Pim and Pom are sorting out the toys.

"你看，乒乓，我们待会儿玩骑士的游戏，我来当骑士……
从凶狠的恶龙手里把外甥女们救出来！"

**'Look Pom, let's play knights
and I'll save the nieces from the fierce dragon!'**

"不嘛，乒乓，我们玩上学的游戏，我来当老师。"

'No Pim, we'll play school and I'll be the teacher.'

女主人的外甥女们要过来玩，她们还要留下喝茶。

女主人做起了十分美味的小蛋糕。

The nieces are coming over to play AND they're staying for tea.

The Lady is baking delicious fairycakes.

嗯，小蛋糕的面糊是世界上最美味的东西。乒乓想要尝一下。
"下去，乒乓，"女主人说，"等一会儿，等外甥女们来了再吃。"

Mmmm... fairycake mix is the best thing in the world. Pim wants a taste.
'Get down Pim,' the Lady says. 'You can have some when the nieces arrive.'

门铃响了。她们来了！
乒乒和乓乓跑向门口。

There's the doorbell. There they are!
Pim and Pom run to the door.

"你好！你好！"外甥女们一边高声尖叫一边往阁楼上跑。
乒乒和乓乓赶紧在她们身后追。

'Hello, Hello!' the nieces scream, as they run up to the attic.
Pim and Pom follow them quickly.

"嘿，外甥女们。看，我是一个骑士！"

'Ha nieces, look, I'm a knight.'

"你看，乒乓，她们正把自己装扮成公主的样子。
她们想要被骑士拯救！"

**'Look Pom, they're dressing up as princesses.
They want to be rescued by the knight!'**

"才不是呢，我们要玩上学的游戏。"乒乓说。

'No, we're going to play school,' says Pom.

可是，看起来外甥女们已经有别的打算了。

But the nieces seem to have a different plan.

"你当小宝宝。"
"不是，我是骑士！"

'You're the baby.'
'No, I'm the knight.'

"把他给我，"另一个外甥女喊道，"他是我的小宝宝！"
小心点儿，外甥女们！

'Give him to me,' shouts the other niece. 'He's my baby!'
Be careful, nieces!

哇！！！

Beeeheeeeh!!!

"好了，现在乖乖躺好！"

'There, be good!'

看哪，外甥女们来了，带着她们的小宝宝乒乓。

There go the nieces with their baby Pim.

哈，那是乒乓老师，他摇响了上课铃。
开始上课了!

Hey! That's Master Pom with the school bell.
School's starting!

"我们玩个更好玩的游戏吧，好人和坏人。
你来当坏人。"外甥女冲着乒乓喊道。

'Let's play goodies and baddies instead. That's more fun.
You're the baddie,' the niece says to Pom.

"你被判一百年监禁，
只能喝水、吃干巴巴的猫粮。"

'You have to stay in prison for a hundred years
with just water and dry cat food.'

女主人的呼喊声传来："茶和小蛋糕好啦！你们来不来啊？"
外甥女们很想吃。她们飞也似的跑下楼。

The Lady calls: 'Tea and fairycakes! Are you coming?'
The nieces love that. They rush down.

等一下，乒乒和乓乓也很想去！

Hey, hang on! Wait for Pim and Pom!

"乒乒骑士，快来救救我吧，
快跳上你那忠诚的摇摆木马。"

**'Oh, Sir Pim, please come and save me,
on your trusty rocking-horse.'**

"救救我，乒乓，我动不了了！
我当然也想吃小蛋糕。"

'Help me Pom, I cannot move!
I want a fairycake of course!'

小蛋糕很快要被吃光了，外甥女们狼吞虎咽，一块接一块。

外甥女们不是真公主。她们是女巫！真扫兴！

The fairycakes are almost finished. Quickly gobbled, one by one.
Those two nieces aren't princesses. They're witches, and this isn't fun!

"乒乒老师，我会来救你的。不要害怕。
乒乒骑士已经出发！"

'Master Pom, I'll come and save you.
Fear not, Sir Pim is on his way!'

"快些跑下楼，乒乓，来不及了，
我们得把外甥女们全部赶走！"

'Come on Pom, no time to lose.
We've got to drive those girls away.'

那两个小女巫太贪心了：
"还剩下最后这几块！全吃掉！"

**Those little witches are so greedy:
'Let's gobble up these ones here!'**

"快点儿，乒乓，
我们要在小蛋糕消失之前冲下楼。"

'Pom, let's rush downstairs before
The fairycakes all disappear.'

当乒乒和乓乓来到楼下时，外甥女们恰好要离开。

"再见，姨妈！"她们大声地喊。

By the time Pim and Pom are downstairs, the nieces run.

'Bye auntie!' they both shout.

看到小外甥女们走了，乒乒和乓乓很高兴。

可是，他们的小蛋糕在哪里呢？

Pim and Pom are happy the nieces are gone.

But where are the fairycakes?

哎呀呀，蛋糕全被她们吃光光了。

Oh, they've eaten all the fairycakes....

"别担心，小猫咪们。"女主人说。

'Don't worry, pussycats,' the Lady says.

"幸好我为你们留了两个。"

'Fortunately I saved two for you.'

"哦耶！是蛋糕！！"

'Hurray! Fairycakes!'